Disney

TSUM TSUM

ULTIMATE STICKER COLLECTION

HOW TO USE THIS BOOK

Read the captions, then find the sticker that best fits the space. (Hint: check the sticker labels for clues!)

•

Don't forget that your stickers can be stuck down and peeled off again.

•

There are lots of fantastic extra stickers for creating your own Disney Tsum Tsum stacks throughout the book.

DK | Penguin Random House

Written and edited by Julia March
Designed by Lynne Moulding, Rhys Thomas, Anna Pond
Jacket designed by Lynne Moulding

First American Edition 2016
First published in the United States in 2016 by DK Publishing
345 Hudson Street, New York, New York 10014

16 17 18 19 10 9 8 7 6 5 4
008-280780-Jan/2016

Published in Great Britain by Dorling Kindersley Limited.

A CIP catalog record for this book is available from the Library of Congress.

DK books are available at special discounts when purchased
in bulk for sales promotions, premiums, fund-raising, or educational use.
For details, contact: DK Publishing Special Markets,
345 Hudson Street, New York, New York 10014
SpecialSales@dk.com

ISBN: 978-1-4654-4422-6

Printed and bound in China

A WORLD OF IDEAS:
SEE ALL THERE IS TO KNOW

www.dk.com

Mickey and friends

Everyone loves Mickey Mouse! The world's most popular mouse has stacks of friends, so naturally, when they get together they make the friendliest stacks of all.

Mickey Mouse
Micky is always happy, but he's happiest of all at the top of a stack.

Pluto
C'mon Pluto! Wherever Mickey Mouse goes, his pet dog Pluto goes too.

Daisy Duck
Elegant Daisy never gets her feathers ruffled, even in the tallest stack.

Donald Duck
If the other Tsum Tsum squash hot-tempered Donald, he's sure to let them know.

Goofy
Watch out when Goofy joins a stack. Clumsy Goofy might bring it tumbling down. Gawsh!

Dale
You can tell Dale from Chip by his light-colored fur and big red nose.

Chip
This cheeky chipmunk and his buddy, Dale, love to play pesky pranks.

Minnie Mouse
Minnie loves stacking, even when her polka-dot bow gets a little crumpled!

Pyramid of pals
Mickey can always rely on his friends for support, like in this pyramid-shaped pile-up.

Animal antics

Whether they have paws, claws, fins, feet, or hooves, there is one thing the animal Tsum Tsum all have in common. They just love to pile up into a pyramid of pets!

Tramp
Lovable mutt Tramp lives on the streets, but he feels right at home in any stack.

Cleo
As part of a stack, Cleo is a fish out of water, but it doesn't bother her one bit!

Pumbaa
This happy warthog has a gassy tummy. Best not be next to him in a stack!

Rajah
Rajah the tiger is a roaring success at his job guarding Princess Jasmine.

Bullseye
Toy horse Bullseye is ready to round up his pals for some stacking. Giddyup!

Pascal

Stacking always makes this clever chameleon turn a happy color!

Crocodile

This toothy croc goes tick-tock. He's eaten Captain Hook's alarm clock.

Cuddly critters

Parisian pussycat Marie has provided the base for a purrfect pile-up for her animal (and alien!) buddies.

Frozen fun

It can get pretty chilly in Arendelle when the snow starts to fall, but the Tsum Tsum know a great way to stay warm. They huddle up and cuddle up together in a nice, snug stack!

Olaf
This chilled-out snowman loves warm hugs. They just make him melt!

Anna
Anna is Elsa's younger sister. She cannot do magic, but she is brave as can be.

Elsa
Queen Elsa has a magical power. When she lets it go, she makes ice and snow.

Chilly chums
Sven, Elsa, Anna, and Kristoff are ready to stack. There's plenty of room on Olaf's back!

Sven
This helpful reindeer pulls Kristoff's sleigh, loaded with stacks of ice.

Pals for Pluto
Use your extra stickers here. Create your own stack of Tsum Tsum pals for Pluto.

Best friends

Everyone likes to be with their best friend, and that includes the Tsum Tsum. It only takes two to be best buddies, but when it comes to stacking, the Tsum Tsum all agree... the more the merrier!

Mickey and Donald
When Donald is in a grouchy mood, his pal Mickey is always there to cheer him up.

Mike and Sulley
Once rival scarers at Monsters University, Mike and Sulley are now firm friends.

Woody and Jessie
Woody and Jessie hit it off the moment they met. They are Wild West besties!

Pinocchio and Jiminy Cricket
When Pinocchio gets into trouble, Jiminy always gets him out of it.

Chip and Dale
Chip and Dale stick together. Two chipmunks can make twice as much mischief as one!

Bambi and Thumper
Thumper is a bold, bouncy rabbit. He is much noisier than his deer pal Bambi.

Pairs of pals
Two by two and side by side, the Tsum Tsum buddies pile up high.

11

Talented Tsum Tsum

Many Tsum Tsum have special talents. Some can even fly, vanish, or make magic... handy when they want to get onto a stack (or out of one) fast.

Queen Elsa
This ice-blonde queen can create flurries of snow and ice. That's so cool!

Dumbo
Getting to the top of a stack is a breeze for Dumbo, the world's only flying elephant.

Rapunzel
This princess's long, golden hair has the magical power to stop people from growing old.

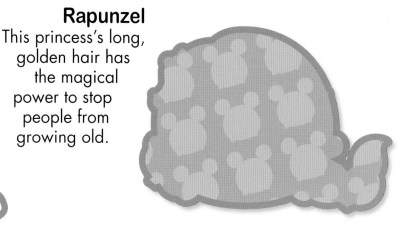

Genie
The blue genie waits in his lamp, ready to grant three wishes to anyone who rubs it.

Tinker Bell
By scattering Fairy Dust on others, Tink can help them fly like she can.

Baymax
Sensors inside robot Baymax help him to intercept radio transmissions.

Maleficent
Bad fairy Maleficent casts evil spells on anyone who snubs her.

Get stacking!
Elsa and Dumbo are starting a stack. Soon, it will be a tower of talented Tsum Tsum.

Cheshire Cat
When it's time to go, this plump cat simply vanishes, leaving just his grin behind.

13

Amazing adventurers

Some Tsum Tsum have had amazing adventures far from home. They've learned to be very brave. Stacking high doesn't scare them one bit!

John Darling
In Neverland, eight-year-old John got mixed up in a scary pirate adventure.

Pinocchio
This living puppet wandered off to look for adventure rather than going to school.

Toy Alien
This toy Alien was parted from his pals after being won as a prize in a vending machine game.

Princess Anna
Brave Anna left the safety of her family castle to search for her sister, Elsa.

Circus elephant
Dumbo was born in a traveling circus. He's been on the move his whole life.

Marie
Cute kitten Marie faced a long journey home after being kidnapped.

Alice
Alice tumbled down a rabbit hole into the weird world of Wonderland.

Stitch
After crash-landing on Hawaii, alien Stitch pretended to be a dog to fit in.

Be brave!
It takes more than a rascal like Stitch to scare Dumbo, Anna, and Marie.

Minnie's friends

Minnie is all alone. Use your extra stickers to create a fun stack of friends for her.

Heroes and villains

Good guys or bad, the Tsum Tsum stack together happily. This is one time when it doesn't matter who comes out on top!

Olaf the hero
Lovable Olaf is proof that being a hero is more about hearts than smarts.

Stinky Pete
This mean old gold prospector is jealous of other, more popular toys.

Hiro Hamada
Clever Hiro creates scientific inventions to defend the city of San Fransokyo.

Captain Hook
Pirate Captain Hook aims to be master of the Seven Seas… by hook or by crook!

Tsum Tsum tower
Heroes and villains work together to make a teetering tower of Tsum Tsum.

Scar

Scar wants to be king of the lions.... and he's ready to claw his way there, if he has to!

Ursula

When sea witch Ursula is stuck in a stack, her potions can't hurt anyone.

Jafar

This sly and sneaky royal advisor is secretly plotting the Sultan's downfall.

19

Royal rulers

They may be royalty, but there's nothing snooty about the Tsum Tsum kings, queens, princes, and princesses. When it's time to stack, they're more than happy to pile in with their loyal subjects.

Jasmine
Princess Jasmine is always hoping for a sneak peek outside the palace walls.

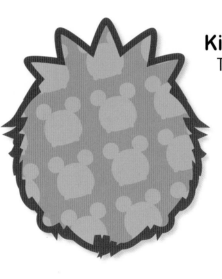

King Triton
The king of Atlantica rages like a stormy sea if anyone disobeys his rules.

Sultan of Agrabah
Finding a husband for Jasmine has given the Sultan the king of headaches!

Mufasa
This noble lion rules the Pride Lands, and is loved by all his subjects.

Princess Aurora

Sleeping Beauty has had enough beauty sleep. She's ready to get stacking.

Cinderella

Cinders went from rags to riches when Prince Charming made her his princess.

Ariel

Little Mermaid Ariel is seventh in line to the undersea throne of Atlantica.

Stately stack

Prince Charming has three princesses to dance with: Anna, Elsa, and Cinderella.

True love

Love is in the air and the Tsum Tsum are getting all romantic with their sweeties. Time to pair up and pile up in a super stack of kissing, cuddling couples.

Mickey and Minnie
It was love at first sight for Mickey and Minnie. They are a perfect mouse match!

Lady and Tramp
Tramp may be just a mutt, but he'll always be Lady's hound dog hero.

Simba and Nala
These cubhood sweethearts grew up to be king and queen of the Pride Lands.

Aurora and Prince Phillip
Phillip's magic kiss woke Aurora from a hundred years of sleep.

Buzz and Jessie
Opposites do attract! Cowgirl Jessie fell head over heels for Buzz the space ranger.

Thumper and Miss Bunny
Cute Miss Bunny really makes Thumper's heart go thump.

Kiss kiss
Mickey and Minnie lean in for a smooch. No wonder the stack looks a bit trembly!

Lonely Lady
Lady cannot wait for her friends to join her. Use your extra stickers to create a super stack.

Work it!

The Tsum Tsum are not afraid of hard work. There are floors to sweep, diamonds to mine, criminals to catch… and more. But they always have plenty of energy left for some stacking fun after hours.

Housemaid
Before Cinderella met her prince, household chores filled her days.

Maximus
This hefty horse is devoted to catching criminals and rescuing Rapunzel.

Circus star
Nobody else has a job like Dumbo's. His flying elephant act is unique.

Sebastian
This cautious crab is a servant of King Triton, and also the court composer.

Dopey
Digging in a diamond mine is hard work, but whistling a tune keeps Dopey cheerful.

Ice harvester
Sven hauls sleds laden with ice all day. It's made him a big, strong reindeer.

Snow White
Snow White sweeps the floor of the Dwarfs' cottage until it is spotless.

Time to stack
Work is over! Now the Tsum Tsum are ready to stack. Sven and Bashful are first on the scene.

Mike
Mike struggled at Monsters Academy, but finally got a good job as a scare assistant.

Down to the woods

The woods can be a quiet, peaceful place. But not when the woodland Tsum Tsum invite Alice and her pals for a stacking picnic. Who says forest creatures are shy?

Bunny girl
Thumper's girlfriend fluffs up her silky fur and ears if they get ruffled.

Little deer
Bambi can be a little unsteady on his feet. Maybe he will take a tumble!

Oyster
The curious Oyster was coaxed from his sea bed to come and join in the fun.

White Rabbit
The pink-eyed rabbit from Wonderland made extra sure he wasn't late today.

Extra guests
Chip and Dale want to join in too… but they might drive everyone nuts with their pranks!

Alice
It's not Wonderland, but Alice thinks this stacking picnic is altogether wonderful.

Smiling cat
The Cheshire Cat is having fun. He isn't going to disappear any time soon.

Noisy rabbit
Noisy Thumper thumps his foot on the ground when he gets excited.

Party time!

It's party time for the Tsum Tsum! When the music starts, so does the fun, with lots of hopping, bopping, and of course stacking. With so many Tsum Tsum together, this could be the biggest stack ever.

Boo
Monsters don't scare little Boo. Neither does dancing at the top of the stack.

Wasabi
Wasabi uses martial arts skills to cut some bold moves in the party stack.

Rafiki
Old age has not slowed down Rafiki the baboon. He still likes to party hard!

All together now...
Here they come, one by one. The party isn't over until everyone's in the stack!

Lotso fun
Even mean old teddy bear Lotso is welcome at the stacking shindig.

Figaro
This cute kitty is happy to party with other cats, dogs, and even fish!

Not so grumpy
Everyone loves to party. Even Grumpy cannot resist joining in the fun.

Goofing around
Goofy cannot wait to show the other Tsum Tsum his goofiest stacking moves.

Buddies for Sven
Don't leave Sven out
in the cold! Use your
extra stickers to create a
stack of pals for him.

Stickers here for pages 2-3

Wise Rafiki

Simba the cub

Dale

Daisy Duck

Mickey Mouse

Goofy

Pluto

Jeff Fungus

Pyramid of pals

Happy Bing Bong

Chip

Mike

Lucifer

Buzz Lightyear

Donald Duck

Minnie Mouse

Stickers here for pages 4-5

Puppet Pinocchio

Young Aladdin

Crocodile

Rajah

Mufasa
the king

Cute Marie

Pascal

Pretty Cinders

Stackable
Sulley

Playful Pluto

Blushing Bashful

Tiny
Thumper

Pumbaa

Bullseye

Randall
Boggs

Jolly
Donald Duck

Cleo

Hamm

Cuddly
critters

Tramp

Stickers here for pages 6-7

Monster smile

Smiling Sultan

Chilly chums

Crazy Goofy

Olaf

Say Boo!

Zazu

Baymax and Sultan

Baymax mech

Anna

Parisian puss

Clever chameleon

Little mermaid

Bing Bong

Fussy Figaro

Elsa

Sven

Pretty Jasmine

Genie of the lamp

Stickers here for pages 10-11

Friendly foursome

Helpful Hiro

Shy Bambi

Chip and Dale

Baby Dumbo

Merryweather

Vanishing cat

Strong Sven

Woody and Jessie

Scary Teddy

Berlioz

Pairs of pals

Crabby Sebastian

Bambi and Thumper

More stickers for pages 10-11

Clever cricket

Sweet Lady

Cute Minnie

Mickey and Donald

Happy MIckey

Pinocchio and Jiminy Cricket

Mike and Sulley

Acting Goofy!

Dainty Marie

Brave Anna

Tumbling Pluto

Smiling Daisy

Fluffy bunny

Mini monster

Stacking pals

Stickers here for pages 12-13

Rapunzel

Sweet Snow White

Maleficent

Tinker Bell

Genie

Happy Pluto

Get stacking!

Queen Elsa

Dumbo

Baymax

Forest friends

Cheshire Cat

Stickers here for pages 14-15

Alice

Bad fairy

Toy Alien

John Darling

© Disney

Pretty Snow White

Princess Anna

Marie

Magic cat

Peas-in-a-Pod

Pinocchio

Circus elephant

Rapunzel's locks

Forest faun

Stitch

Tiny Tinkers

Winking Anna

Playful Dale

Clever Alice

Be brave!

Stickers here for pages 18-19

Ursula

Little Lady

Scar

Cheeky Chip

Olaf the hero

Stinky Pete

Pink-eyed rabbit

All smiles!

Tsum Tsum tower

Jafar

Cute Cleo

Bold Buzz

Cuddly reindeer

Kind Anna

Captain Hook

Queen of ice

Hiro Hamada

Stickers here for pages 20-21

Ariel

Smiling Stitch

Lovely Snow White

King Triton

Jasmine

Mufasa

Nala

Tiger Lily

Funny Olaf

Cinderella

Princess Aurora

Sultan of Agrabah

Elsa crowned

Lilo

Stately stack

Stickers here for pages 22-23

Cute cubs

Courageous Anna

Mickey and Minnie

Rajah the tiger

Just Sven

Thumper and Miss Bunny

Timon

Buzz and Jessie

Hiro the hero

Royal couple

Lady and Tramp

Tricky trio

Sleepy

Stack of Olafs

More stickers here for pages 22-23

Mouse couple

Scuttle

Simba and Nala

Little Oyster

Aurora and Prince Phillip

Funny bunnies

Sweet Cinderella

Dear Dopey

Evil fairy

Faithful Bullseye

Trusty Tramp

Worried Jiminy

Mini Mike

Lotso and Jessie

Popular mouse

Kiss kiss

Perfect pooch

© Disney

© Disney/Pixar

Stickers here for pages 26-27

Maximus

Sebastian

Sulley the scarer

Happy Hamm

Mike

Woody

Time to stack

Ice harvester

Circus star

Housemaid

Dopey

Furry Figaro

Snow White

Stickers here for pages 28-29

Smiling cat

Bunny girl

Dapper Donald

Oyster

Noisy rabbit

Pyramid of pals

Little deer

Anger

Flying elephant

Little Figaro

Alice

Leaping Lady

Sweet Cinders

White Rabbit

Extra guests

Stickers here for pages 30-31

Boo

Friendly trio

Dancing Mickey

Disgust

Figaro

Wasabi

Lotso fun

Stinky Pete and Lucifer

Not so grumpy

Stacking singles

Beautiful bunny

Kitten Marie

Elsa forever

Hopping Stitch

Jaunty Donald

Goofing around

Rafiki

Merry Minnie

Lovable Dale

Super stack

So much Anger!

Let's party!

Extra stickers

Extra stickers

Extra stickers

Extra stickers

Extra stickers

Extra stickers

Extra stickers

Extra stickers

Extra stickers

© Disney
© Disney/Pixar
© Disney
© Disney
© Disney
© Disney
© Disney
© Disney
© Disney
© Disney/Pixar
© Disney
© Disney
© Disney
© Disney
© Disney
© Disney
© Disney

Extra stickers

© Disney

© Disney

© Disney

© Disney

© Disney

© Disney/Pixar

© Disney/Pixar

© Disney

© Disney

© Disney

© Disney

© Disney

© Disney

© Disney

Extra stickers

© Disney

Extra stickers

Extra stickers

Extra stickers

Extra stickers

© Disney

© Disney

© Disney

© Disney

© Disney

© Disney

© Disney/Pixar

© Disney

© Disney

© Disney

© Disney

© Disney

© Disney

Extra stickers

© Disney/Pixar

© Disney/Pixar

© Disney

© Disney

© Disney/Pixar

© Disney/Pixar

© Disney

© Disney/Pixar

© Disney

© Disney

© Disney

© Disney

© Disney

© Disney

© Disney

© Disney/Pixar

© Disney/Pixar

Extra stickers

Extra stickers